ILISA, THE GILDMASTER

ILISA, THE GILDMASTE[R] HAD MORE MONEY THA[N] COULD EVER SPEND, [BUT] HE WAS TIGHT-FIST[ED]

1

UNLESS I EAT THEM SOMEWHERE ELSE...

COME HERE.

GO AND BUY SOME JALEBIS FROM THE SWEETMEAT SHOP.

YES, MASTER.

BUT DON'T BRING THEM HERE... TAKE THEM TO THE BUSHES NEAR THE LAKE. I'LL WAIT THERE FOR YOU.

AS ILISA WAS MAKING HIS ELABORATE PLANS, A MAN WHO WAS HIS EXACT LIKENESS PRESENTED HIMSELF BEFORE THE KING.

WHAT BRINGS YOU HERE, GILDMASTER?

MAHARAJ, I HAVE COME TO SEEK YOUR PERMISSION...

... TO GIVE AWAY SOME OF MY GREAT WEALTH.

WHAT!

4

IF HE COMES HERE, BEAT HIM AND DRIVE HIM AWAY.

YES, MASTER.

IT'S A SHAME THAT ILISA'S WIFE SHOULD WEAR SUCH DOWDY CLOTHES.

!

GO TO THE MARKET AND BUY WHATEVER YOU WANT... BUY SOMETHING FOR THE CHILDREN TOO.

ARE... ARE YOU ALL RIGHT?

I'VE NEVER FELT BETTER.

IT'S JUST THAT I AM IN A GENEROUS MOOD TODAY.

TELL EVERYONE YOU MEET THAT I AM GIVING AWAY HALF MY WEALTH TO THE POOR AND NEEDY.

HE HAS TAKEN LEAVE OF HIS SENSES, BUT I'D BETTER BUY SOMETHING FOR MYSELF BEFORE HE CHANGES HIS MIND.

SOON, PEOPLE BEGAN TO STREAM INTO ILISA'S HOUSE.

MASTER... MASTER...

COME IN, COME IN.

PICK UP WHATEVER YOU WANT AND GO.

WHATEVER WE WANT!

OUT OF MY WAY!

HE MAY CHANGE HIS MIND ANY MOMENT.

YES, WE ALL KNOW WHAT A MISER HE IS.

TALES OF MISERS

ONE MAN WORKED MORE METHODICALLY THAN THE OTHERS. INSTEAD OF RUSHING INTO THE HOUSE, HE CHOSE A BULLOCK-CART FOR HIMSELF...

...LOADED IT WITH VALUABLES FROM THE STOREROOM...

...AND DROVE AWAY SINGING THE PRAISES OF HIS BENEFACTOR.

THERE IS NO ONE GREATER THAN THE NOBLE ILISA!

I'VE GOT A FINE PAIR OF BULLOCKS, AND A CARTLOAD OF TREASURE.

MAY ILISA LIVE A THOUSAND YEARS!

WHAT!

SOMEONE'S PRAISING ME!

7

YOU ARE ALL GOING TO PAY DEARLY FOR THIS!

I'LL COME BACK WITH THE KING'S MEN.

ILISA RUSHED TO THE PALACE

MAHARAJ, I AM BEING LOOTED!

PEOPLE ARE CARRYING AWAY MY PROPERTY!

BUT GILDMASTER...

...YOU YOURSELF CAME HERE AND ASKED FOR MY PERMISSION TO GIVE AWAY YOUR WEALTH!

!!

MAHARAJ, HAVE YOU EVER KNOWN ME TO GIVE AWAY ANYTHING?

SOME IMPOSTOR HAS TAKEN MY PLACE!

I WILL HAVE HIM BROUGHT HERE.

WHEN THE IMPERSONATOR WAS BROUGHT TO THE PALACE, THE KING AND HIS COURTIERS FOUND THEMSELVES GAZING AT TWO MEN WHO LOOKED IDENTICAL IN ALL RESPECTS.

NOW WHO IS WHO?

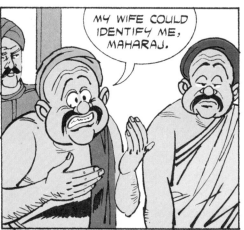

MY WIFE COULD IDENTIFY ME, MAHARAJ.

BUT WHEN ILISA'S WIFE WAS BROUGHT TO THE PALACE AND ASKED TO IDENTIFY HER HUSBAND—

THAT'S MY HUSBAND!

UNGRATEFUL WOMAN! AFTER ALL I'VE DONE FOR YOU!

NOW WHO... WHAT... WHY, MY BARBER OF COURSE!

MAHARAJ, MY BARBER COULD IDENTIFY ME!

THE BARBER WAS BROUGHT TO THE PALACE AND ASKED TO IDENTIFY ILISA.

I'LL HAVE TO EXAMINE THEIR HEADS, MAHARAJ.

THIS IS UNCANNY!

I CANNOT IDENTIFY THE GILDMASTER, MAHARAJ.

WHAT DO YOU MEAN!

I HAVE A WART ON MY HEAD. HAVE YOU FORGOTTEN?

YOU HAVE A WART... BUT SO DOES HE!

EVEN MY WIFE HAS IDENTIFIED HIM AS HER HUSBAND!

I'LL BE THROWN OUT OF MY OWN HOUSE... AND I'LL LOSE ALL MY WEALTH... OOOH!

HE HAS FAINTED!

THROW SOME WATER ON HIM.

WHEN ILISA WAS RESTORED TO HIS SENSES—

I SHALL NOT FRIGHTEN YOU ANY MORE.

I AM YOUR FATHER... COME DOWN FROM HEAVEN.

F-FATHER!

ALL THE WEALTH YOU POSSESS IS MINE. I WAS GENEROUS TO THE POOR AND NEEDY...

...BUT YOU HAVE PUT ALL MY WEALTH UNDER LOCK AND KEY AND IT IS OF NO USE TO ANYONE!

I WILL TAKE AWAY ALL MY WEALTH IF YOU PERSIST IN SUCH BEHAVIOUR!

I...I WON'T, FATHER!

GIVE ME ANOTHER CHANCE!

THEN ILISA'S FATHER RETURNED TO THE CELESTIAL WORLD...

...AND ILISA RETURNED HOME...

...A GENEROUS AND CONSIDERATE MAN.

KESIYA

LONG AGO, THERE LIVED A MISER KESIYA. HE WAS THE KING'S TREASURER. ONE DAY AS HE WAS GOING HOME—

HE'S EATING POODAS.

IT'S SUCH A LONG TIME SINCE I HAVE EATEN POODAS.

I COULD ASK MY WIFE TO MAKE SOME... BUT THE COST!

WHEN KESIYA REACHED HOME—

YOU LOOK SAD. WHAT'S THE MATTER?

NOTHING.

TELL ME WHAT'S WRONG. IS THE KING ANGRY WITH YOU FOR SOME REASON?

NO.

HAVE ANY OF THE SERVANTS ASKED FOR A RAISE?

OH, NO!

THEY'RE ALL GOOD PEOPLE.

WHAT'S THE MATTER, THEN?

WELL, IF YOU MUST KNOW... I HAVE A CRAVING FOR POODAS.

POODAS?

IS THAT ALL? I'LL MAKE SOME FOR YOU RIGHT AWAY.

IN FACT, I'LL MAKE ENOUGH FOR THE WHOLE NEIGHBOURHOOD!

WHAT!

HAVE YOU TAKEN LEAVE OF YOUR SENSES, WOMAN!

I....
I....

ALL RIGHT, I'LL MAKE JUST ENOUGH FOR US.

FOR US?

FOR THE CHILDREN, FOR YOU AND FOR ME.

LEAVE THE CHILDREN OUT.

THEY MAY NOT CARE FOR POODAS.

THEN I'LL MAKE JUST ENOUGH FOR THE TWO OF US.

YOU DON'T REALLY WANT TO EAT POODAS, DO YOU?

ER... WELL...

I THOUGHT AS MUCH. MAKE JUST ENOUGH FOR ME.

WAIT!

WE MUST BE CAREFUL. IF YOU MAKE THE POODAS IN THE KITCHEN, THE AROMA WILL ATTRACT THE NEIGHBOURS...

...AND THEN WE'LL HAVE TO GIVE THEM SOME. I'LL TELL YOU WHAT WE'LL DO.

WE'LL TAKE EVERYTHING WE NEED UP TO THE TERRACE AND YOU CAN MAKE THE POODAS UP THERE.

SO KESIYA AND HIS WIFE, CARRIED THE UTENSILS AND INGREDIENTS REQUIRED TO MAKE THE POODAS...

21

DO YOU THINK YOU CAN GET A POODA BY HOVERING UP THERE?

I WOULDN'T GIVE YOU ONE EVEN IF YOU WERE STANDING ON THIS TERRACE.

DO... DO YOU THINK I'LL GIVE YOU A POODA JUST BECAUSE WE ARE STANDING ON THE SAME TERRACE?

I WOULDN'T GIVE YOU ONE EVEN IF YOU WERE STANDING BESIDE ME.

MAKE A SMALL ONE FOR HIM.

BUT KESIYA'S WIFE FOUND THAT SHE COULD NOT MAKE A SMALL POODA FOR THE UNINVITED GUEST.

THAT'S TURNED OUT EVEN BIGGER.

I CAN'T HELP IT!

THE PASTE KEEPS ON SPREADING OVER THE WHOLE PAN. THERE'S SOMETHING VERY STRANGE GOING ON HERE.

YOU'RE JUST A BAD COOK, THAT'S ALL!

GIVE HIM THAT ONE ON TOP AND LET HIM GO AWAY.

THEY ARE ALL STUCK TOGETHER.

PULL!

MY WIFE WAS RIGHT. SOMETHING VERY STRANGE IS GOING ON HERE.

IT IS CLEAR THAT WE ARE NOT DEALING WITH AN ORDINARY MAN.

YOU CAN HAVE ALL THE POODAS, RESPECTED SIR.

SIT AND EAT.

I WANT THEM NOT FOR MYSELF...

...BUT FOR MY LORD BUDDHA AND HIS DISCIPLES. THEY ARE WAITING FOR ME.

BUDDHA!

F-FORGIVE ME! I DID NOT KNOW...

COME WITH ME IF YOU WISH TO MEET HIM.

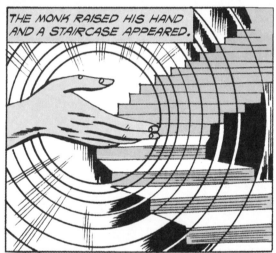

THE MONK RAISED HIS HAND AND A STAIRCASE APPEARED.

KESIYA AND HIS WIFE WENT DOWN IT...

...TILL FINALLY—

HERE WE ARE.

THE LORD BUDDHA.

BUDDHA ACCEPTED THE OFFERING OF POODAS AND THEY WERE DISTRIBUTED AMONG HIS MONKS.

KESIYA AND HIS WIFE TOO GOT THEIR SHARE.

THIS IS THE FIRST TIME I HAVE SHARED MY FOOD WITH STRANGERS.

AND STRANGELY, I FEEL HAPPY...ER, WHAT ARE YOU STARING AT?

THE POODAS.

EVERYONE HAS EATEN BUT THE TRAY IS AS FULL AS BEFORE.

NEVER HAVE I SEEN SUCH A WONDER! THIS IS THE GREATEST DAY OF MY LIFE!

KESIYA RETURNED HOME A CHANGED MAN.

WIFE, TOMORROW YOU WILL MAKE POODAS FOR THE WHOLE NEIGHBOURHOOD.

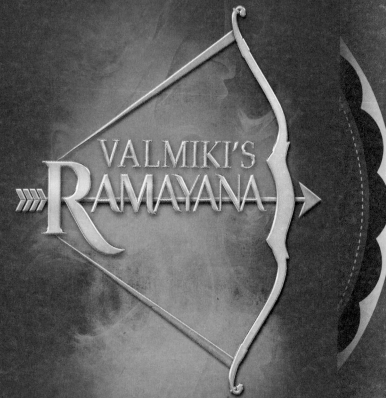

21 Inspiring Stories of Courage

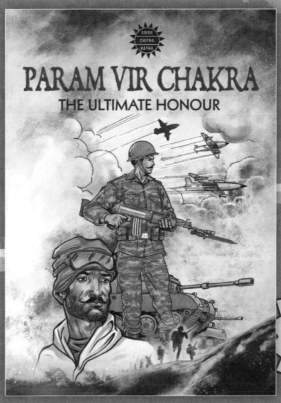

MRP ₹449/-